The Lost Diary of

Leonardo's Paint Mixer

The Lost Diary of Leonardo's Paint Mixer

Found by Alex Parsons
Illustrated by George Hollingworth

Collins
An imprint of HarperCollins*Publishers*

First published in Great Britain by Collins in 1999

Collins is an imprint of HarperCollins*Publishers* Ltd,
77-85 Fulham Palace Road, Hammersmith, London W6 8JB

The HarperCollins website address is www.**fire**and**water**.com

1 3 5 7 9 8 6 4 2

Text copyright © Alex Parsons 1999
Illustrations copyright © George Hollingworth 1999
Cover illustration copyright © Martin Chatterton 1999

ISBN 0 00 694590 2

The author and illustrators assert the moral right to be
identified as the author and illustrators of the work.

Printed and bound in Great Britain by
Caledonian International Book Manufacturing Ltd, Glasgow, G64

MESSAGE TO READERS

Luigi Cannelloni's story of life among the Colourful Set in Renaissance Italy has been sniffed at by art historians ever since his tatty notebook was discovered in an antique terracotta pot used as an umbrella stand at *Leonardo's*, an aptly named Italian restaurant somewhere in London.

Professor Spottafake, an eminent art historian, had the cheek to question the possibility of an early 16th century Italian manuscript turning up in a late 20th century pasta joint. After a few glasses of Chianti, he dismissed the 'Diary' as the drunken ramblings of someone waiting too long for an order of Spaghetti Bolognese.

But it takes an expert in more than art history to tell the difference between age spots and gravy stains, and this is where one of *Leonardo's* regular customers, Alex Parsons, comes in.

Thanks to Ms Parsons, we can all now enjoy the authentic flavour of 16th century Italy, and dine out on delicious, mouth-watering tales of flaking frescos, power-crazy popes, pushy patrons and that genius who was Leonardo da Vinci.

The Verrocchio Workshop, Florence, 1470

Mamma mia! The work, the backbreaking work! My friend Paolo got himself apprenticed to a baker. The hours! The heat! The flour! The customers! It was a terrible warning. Me? When a job was advertised in an artists' workshop, I pictured an easy life.

"Luigi Cannelloni," I said to myself (because that is my name), "what a cushy number! All you're gonna have to do is waft around looking arty, clean a few paintbrushes, help the gorgeous models off with their clothes, serve wine and cakes to the customers and sweep the place up a bit when they've all gone home." How wrong can you be?

Signore Verrocchio, The Master, is my boss. He is actually the most important artist working in Florence. The trouble with him is that there isn't any commission* he'll turn down – he'll work for anyone.

If one of the Medici family (they're the ruling family of Florence, so you don't mess with them) take it into their heads to order a sculpture of a full-sized man on a horse, "*No problema*!" says The Master. "I'll send the boy to pick up ten tons of bronze."

* an order for work.

If they want their ceilings painted with God and all his angels, "*No problema*! I'll send the boy round to put up the scaffolding."

If they want a marble statue for their uncle's tomb, "*No problema*! I'll send the boy up to the quarry to hack out half a mountain and run home with it on his back."

We have lots of artists in this workshop, but only one genius. Even The Master admits to this. The genius's name is Leonardo da Vinci.

He's quite different from the other artists here. I mean obviously they can all draw and stuff like that, and they can all paint, but when Leonardo paints or draws someone, you get the feeling the figure is alive, as if the skin is warm to the touch and that you know who they are.

Take the other day. The Master's been working on this painting of the *Baptism of Christ* and he wanted the figure of an angel in there, so not being particularly good at painting angels, he asked Leonardo to paint one in.

Bravissimo! Leonardo's painting was like a real angel – so beautiful that it made the other figures look very flat and ordinary.

Surprise, surprise! The Master has announced that he will be concentrating on the sculpture side of the business, and is leaving the painted works to other artists in the group. I wonder why?

Florence, 1471

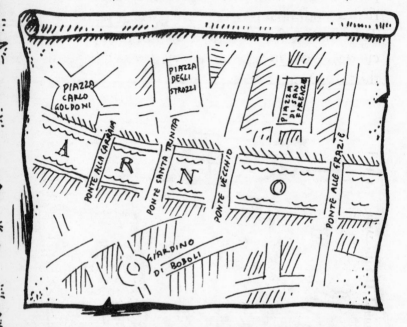

Florence is a very interesting place to live. We have our own currency*, the gold Florin, which is valid the world over, or so I am told. We have our own rulers, the powerful Medici family who made their fortune out of banking and inventing accountancy. As a result they have their own *palazzo***, which is built four-square around a courtyard. The outside has only ten windows, is rather forbidding, and looks like a military fortress.

* money.
** palace.

Now why would a family with money coming out of their *orecchie* * live in such a place? Well, this is probably why they are the richest and most powerful family in these parts. They built it this way so that we poor humble citizens wouldn't pass by every day and hate them for being rich.

But I have been inside, delivering sculptures and paintings, and I can tell you, their wealth is knee-buckling.

* ears.

Florence, 1472

The young Leonardo is not just a painter of pretty faces. He wants to know how everything works and then make it work better. Take the dome of Florence Cathedral, for example. The workshop has a commission to sculpt a golden sphere to fit right on top of the cathedral dome.

Instead of spending time sculpting in the workshop, Leonardo is poring over the plans of the cathedral with the architect Brunelleschi. He's made hundreds of drawings of the cranes being used to hoist up the stones. His sketchbooks are full of gears, axles, rollers and pivots. I think he'd rather be an engineer than an artist.

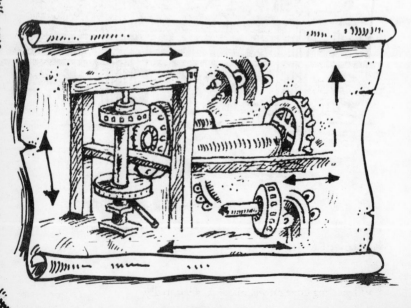

Leonardo also spends a lot of time gazing at a fresco* in the Church of Santa Maria Novella. All the painters in our Workshop have an opinion about this painting of *The Trinity*. The artist, Masaccio, drew the vaulted ceiling in the background using *mathematics*, not guesswork like the rest of us. It's spooky because it makes everything look so real.

This may well be the way art is going. Artists today are talking about being real and using real models and all that kind of stuff. It's the fashion to sniff at the artists of the past and put them down as primitive decorators. I can sniff with the best of them.

* wall painting done on wet plaster and left to dry.

Florence, Winter 1475

Leonardo and I went out for a drink after work the other day and I got to know our resident genius a bit better. He was born in Anchiano, a little village near Vinci. His mother, whom he has never met (to speak to, I mean), was a peasant girl called Caterina. His papa is Piero da Vinci, a successful lawyer who works here in Florence. Obviously Papa da Vinci is a bit of a ladies' man as Leonardo's already had four step-mothers, all of them lavishing love and attention on him, so he's a bit of a Momma's boy four times over.

Leonardo's a very charming bloke, no doubt about it. Easy to talk to, and generous too. And he certainly stands out from the crowd. Everyone else wanders around town in long beige robes, but not Leonardo. He wears short velvet doublets* and bright blue tights, a very colourful chap. He doesn't seem to have much interest in girls, which is a bit odd. I found myself mentioning my wife Giulia rather a lot and banging my tankard about in a manly way.

* tight-fitting jackets.

Florence, 1476

Have I got a problem! Leonardo is leaving The Master's workshop and has asked me to go with him to work as his assistant.

Now, I could stay here at this painting and sculpture factory for the rest of my life: the hours are long, the people nice but dull, the boss a bit moody, the work hard, but it's regular pay.

Or I could put my life in the hands of this eccentric genius, who will either amount to nothing or become the most famous painter in the world. And if he does, my diary will become a world-beating bestseller the minute someone sorts out printing.

Hmmm. And Leonardo does hang out with a rather *colourful* bunch of people. What will my friends think? Oh well, you only live once!

Let me tell you something about rivalry. You wouldn't believe the flouncing that goes on when the Colourful Set meet up at the marketplace.

My technique is better than your technique.

My colours are truer to life.

My drapery is more convincing than yours.

My patron has better taste than your patron.

"Hey guys!" I am tempted to say. "Who do you think you are? And as for your patrons*, they may not know art when they see it, but they know what they like."

* people who sponsor artists.

Florence, January 1477

I will say this for my new master, Leonardo. He does know his paints. He knows how to grind up rocks and stones and mud to make his colours. He knows how to prepare a canvas, or a panel of wood, or a plaster wall. He knows how to cast bronze and to make armatures*. He knows his geometry and his chemistry. In fact there's very little he doesn't know.

And I'll tell you something else about him. He starts a million jobs and FINISHES NONE OF THEM! I can see this may well drive me mad.

* internal frames which support sculptures.

He's very keen on oil paint at the moment.
This is a method of mixing paints with a mixture
of boiled linseed oil and nut oil so that pictures
dry in the shade. Normally, you see, we put
them out in the sun to dry, which can often
make the wooden panels split.

Though I say it myself, I am very good at
mixing paint. But it is not an easy job. For blue,
I have to pound up lapis lazuli (it comes in
lumps of precious blue stone). For red I squeeze
roots of the madder plant and grind up the
mineral vermilion. For yellow I use the urine of
Indian cows fed on mango leaves, and I've heard
some colourmen (that's the official name for my
profession) make a brown using ground-up
Egyptian mummies. But not me.

Leonardo says my oil paint makes skin tones luminous and hair like silk, and gives him total control over light and shade, plus you don't see the brush strokes. So I dash about like a mad thing, pounding rocks, mixing oils, burning charcoal, making glue and stirring varnish. And what's he doing? Helping with all the mad activity that he's started? No, he's gazing into the middle distance looking for inspiration. Inspiration! What use is inspiration when the glue pot's boiling over?

Florence, Spring 1477

The models are a bit of a pain in the *posteriore*.
Leonardo gets all kinds of people to pose for
him, and I thought I'd be having a happy time
draping beautiful girls in skimpy bits of silk.
But, needless to say, most of his models are
beautiful young men with curly hair. And
between ourselves, they're a stroppy lot.

But that's not the worst part. He's also taken to
filling the studio with toothless old peasants. He
gets them to come in and sit about having a
laugh. When I've pushed the last old crank out
of the door, he gets out his sketchbook and
draws frantically from memory. I don't know
why he bothers. How many altarpieces or
portraits of important people have you seen
with a gaggle of grinning peasants in the
foreground? None. Art patrons don't want to
see the rough side of life. They just want
painters to make them look good in portraits
and paint the usual religious paintings to make
them feel holy.

There is a bit of a change in the air. When Florence's artistic set gather round for a bit of a natter, the talk is not of how many metres of mural they can knock out in a month, but how they can bring real emotion and feeling into their pictures.

And what's more, they're all getting a bit temperamental, talking about being creative and waiting for inspiration. Inspiration? There's that word again. There was a time when being an artist was a job just like any other.

Now they're getting worried about being seen as just craftsmen, when they think – well, Leonardo thinks – that painting and sculpture are up there with the highest achievements of man.

Actually Leonardo often goes a bit further than this, as he privately thinks he's on the way to understanding the laws of Nature. When he's cracked it, he'll be a bit of a rival to The Creator Himself.

Florence, Winter 1478

I suspected it before, but now I *know* that Leonardo's lost the plot. We've got this rich patron we've been bowing and scraping to for weeks who wants some portrait or other. What's my boss doing? He's scribbling away in his notebooks inventing things. As if I didn't have enough to do, he's got me sewing together animal skins, filling them with air and strapping them to my feet. And now I'm supposed to be able to walk on water.

"No way, Leonardo," I said. "Keep your inventions in your notebooks, Maestro. We are not, repeat *not*, going in for any practical experiments."

It was just as well I put my foot down (although it's quite hard to stamp meaningfully with an inflated sheepskin tied to your shoe), because his next invention was a contraption for breathing underwater.

Florence, 30th December 1479

Leonardo has been neglecting his commissions. I said to him yesterday, "Maestro, are you sure you know which side your *panini** is buttered on? You can't keep upsetting the people who run this town (that's the Medici family, in case you haven't been paying attention). Have you seen what they've done to poor old Bernardo Bandini?"

Now I admit Bernardo was more of a big-time traitor than an artist who failed to deliver on time, but nevertheless, it's an example of the way the Medicis behave towards people who irritate them. They've strung the poor guy up from a window in the Palazzo Vecchio.

* type of Italian bread.

Any normal person would have shuddered a bit and got on with his commissions quick smart, but not Leonardo. He grabbed his sketchbook and rushed off to the Palazzo Vecchio to draw poor old Bernardo's final agony.

I've been peeking in his notebooks and I know he's been sneaking down to the local morgue and drawing *dead* people too.

Florence, Spring 1480

Well, we're not getting much done in the way of paintings, but Leonardo's collection of sketchbooks is growing. He's done some lovely nature drawings. He's also been telling me some more stories from his childhood.

Apparently he would spend hours and hours in his father's vineyard watching the lizards, crickets, grasshoppers and butterflies going about their business in the fields. He loved everything that grew, or flew, or crawled, and he used to take himself off to the marketplace with his pocket money, buy a cage of birds and then let them fly free!

"I gave them back their lost liberty!" said Leonardo.

"You gave away your pocket money," said I.

Leonardo's first painting was a dragon on the shield belonging to one of his father's peasants. It was a dragon inspired by the lizards he'd been watching, and he surrounded the image with bats and things to make it look ugly and frightening. I made a mental note to pop back and find that peasant. Who knows what the first daubings of a great artist might be worth some day?

Florence, 1481

So this great artist – Leonardo da Vinci – what has he actually painted up to now? Not a whole heap. There's an unfinished *Adoration of the Magi** which hasn't been coloured in yet (if I know Leonardo, it probably never will be), a portrait or two and a couple of *Madonnas*.

There's no doubt the boy's got talent. He doesn't see the people and the things he paints as flat shapes you draw an outline around. He sees them as 3-D** bodies that are there all right, but you only get to see them because of the light that falls on them. I don't know if I'm making myself clear, but his people kind of come at you from the shadows.

* Wise Men.
** three dimensional.

And he does like to make life difficult for himself. Any normal artist would be quite happy to sign his pictures in a normal way: Leonardo da Vinci. Not hard. But he doesn't do that, it would be far too simple. He writes: Leonardo da Vinci, which only makes sense if you hold a mirror up to it. In fact he's started writing in his notebooks in this tiny spidery mirror-writing. "Why?" I asked him. "It makes life more of a challenge," he replied.

Personally I think he's being coy, or secretive. Maybe he thinks his ideas might get stolen. Or maybe he doesn't want The Church to understand anything if they should happen to take a peek at his notebooks. Priests never like anyone who tries to find out how God puts things together.

Or perhaps it's just that he's left-handed and so he's worked out a way of moving his pen over the page so his writing doesn't get smudged.

Florence, 1482

Leonardo is talking about moving to Milan. I wonder why? There aren't as many great artists in Milan, which could have something to do with it. So could the fact that the top man in Milan, Lodovico Sforza, is looking for a sculptor who can cast a three-times-life-sized bronze sculpture of a man on a horse in memory of his dear departed Papa.

Leonardo knows how to sculpt horses and how to cast bronze, but no one has ever cast a horse as big as this before. That's probably why Leonardo has accepted the commission – there's nothing my boss likes better than a challenge. So it looks like I'll be up to my ears in molten bronze for the next few years. *Andiamo allora!* * I'd better get packing.

* Let's go!

Milan, 1483

We are living in a very fine apartment in one of Lodovico Sforza's palaces, and very nice it is too. Leonardo's made plenty of new friends. There's Francesco, a military engineer; a mathematician called Luca Paciloli; and a guy named Marcantonio who spends his days cutting up dead bodies – it's called studying anatomy, apparently.

Not a very arty bunch you could say, but they're up till all hours 'exchanging ideas'. Leonardo is now wildly keen on dead bodies, maths and military engineering, and is teaching himself Latin to keep up with the upper classes. How does that rhyme go? 'Latin is a language as dead as dead can be, it killed the ancient Romans and now it's killing me.' Doesn't sound like much fun, but there's no accounting for taste.

"The horse, the horse," I keep saying rather feebly. "We must get on with it, otherwise Lodovico will be saying *arrivederci**.*"

"Armoured cars! Thirty-three-barrelled gun carriages!" he mutters back. He's forgotten about the horse!

As it happens, Lodovico is a bit preoccupied with war, as Milan seems to be under constant threat from Venice. Leonardo has now offered his services as a designer of military and naval weaponry *and* as architect, painter, drainage engineer (no kidding!) and (finally) sculptor.

Terrifico! Where do I, a humble paint pigment crusher and pourer of molten metal, come into all this? Can't the guy just concentrate on one thing? Who does he think he is, Renaissance Man**?

* goodbye.
** someone who knows everything about the arts and the sciences.

Milan, April 1483

Yes! Someone has asked Leonardo to paint an altarpiece! You always know where you are with an altarpiece. Actually, he shares the commission with a couple of other painters. I'm sure the church is acting on good advice here, knowing if it was up to Leonardo alone, they'd probably get their painting some time in the 17th century.

But there you go, you never know where you are with The Maestro. Just when you think he's going to rush off and re-arrange Milan's drainage system, leaving you to explain about the empty panels above the altar, he comes up with two paintings and they're both absolutely stunning. The other guys never got to pick up a brush.

Milan, 1485

The Maestro's an absolute genius, but I think he's a few pigments short of a palette with this armoured car. It's like a huge metal pie, and under the crust of the pie eight guys are supposed to crank the wheels and fire the guns. How do they see where they're going? How do they move this massive, heavy contraption across the average muddy battlefield? How soon would the soldiers inside the tin pie go deaf from the sound of gunfire?

Give him his due, though. Leonardo closed his notebook the other day and got on with a painting of Lodovico's mistress, a pretty girl called Cecilia. Obviously Leonardo's learned how to please his patron, and instead of calling the painting *Hey Everyone! This is Lodovico's Girlfriend!* he's called it *Lady with an Ermine*. Very discreet.

Milan, 1488

Cathedrals, cathedrals, cathedrals! Now he's got a thing about architecture and he's dreaming up vast vaulted cathedrals with domes everywhere. They're all very geometrical and symmetrical, as you might expect.

He was only asked to design a covered passageway for Milan Cathedral. But you might have known he wouldn't stop there.

I think the authorities at Milan Cathedral were a bit spooked too, when instead of a little passageway, they got designs for a dozen cathedrals, plus engineering drawings, plus a long lecture on how the proportion of a dome was like the proportion of a skull and how a good strong building was like a healthy body.

I think they will think he's mad and I think they will say 'thanks but no thanks' to his cathedrals.

Milan, 1489

We've been in Milan for eight years now, but Leonardo still hasn't done the horse for Lodovico. But among all the plans for new cathedrals, the allegorical drawings* (did I mention the philosophy?), the sonnets (did I mention the poetry?) and the essays on painting (did I mention the writing?), we finally have some drawings of a horse! Lodovico will be pleased.

* drawings which explain ideas, e.g. a skull meaning death, or a dog meaning faithfulness.

We've got great snorting, pawing beasts trampling on people (very difficult to balance) and proud walking horses (easier to balance and a lot less controversial). Eight years into the commission, this is a good start, although Lodovico might be disappointed to discover that as yet there's no drawing of the rider. Those of us with long memories will not need reminding that the original idea of the monument was to glorify the memory of Lodovico's Papa, Francesco, not his horse. But try telling that to Leonardo.

Milan, 1490

Now Leonardo has yet another job at Lodovico's court. He's the grand master of fun and games, pageants and processions, fireworks and feasting, and is known as the Official Artificer. What jolly fun. It's all costume fittings and seating plans at the studio now, and if you asked me to lay my hands on a tin of paint or a block of marble, I wouldn't know where to look.

Lodovico's nephew is marrying Isabel of Aragon and Lodo wants to party. The theme is Paradise – and why not? Leonardo has designed costumes that make the performers look like the planets, kind of yellow and round. They hang around, as planets do, and then speak words of praise in honour of the bride. What she will make of it I don't know, but it's costing Lodo a packet.

Leonardo's made a mechanical lion! He made it to honour the visit of the King of France to Milan. Funny that. Seeing how they are always at war, I would have thought Lodovico would greet the King of France with a barrage from a thirty-three-barrelled revolving gun, but that's politics for you. This lion had some kind of clockwork mechanism inside. It walked forward a few paces (it did! it did!), a trap door in its belly was released, and *whoosh!* Out fell a thousand lilies. *Magnifico*!

Milan, April 1490

It will come as no surprise to you, dear Diary, that Lodovico is still waiting for his horse. Apparently he wrote to the Medici family at the end of last year asking them if they knew anyone else who a) could make the horse and b) might be slightly quicker at it than the esteemed Leonardo da Vinci.

This did speed The Maestro up. He's actually decided to start work on the horse! *Fantastico!* It's the reason we came here nine years ago, after all.

Milan, 1491

Leonardo has just drawn a brilliant diagram. I actually posed for the first sketch in my underpants, but then he sent me out to find a fair, curly-haired young man who didn't mind taking his clothes off, so he could complete the drawing.

(Apparently, these young male models are not naturally blond. They are often up all night with the bleach bottle and the curling tongs.)

The diagram is based on the ideas of the Roman architect Vitruvius, who had a theory that the human body could be used as a basis for proportion. Leonardo has got out his geometry set and proved it. Your head is a fifth of your body height and so on. I did point out that not all people were perfect. Some people have long backs and short legs, for instance. But Leonardo is only interested in perfection.

Milan, 1492

Leonardo is spending a lot of time drawing horses now, which is good, because when Lodovico's men pop round from time to time asking anxiously about the progress of the monument, I can say, with my hand on my heart, "Tell your boss everything's fine, he's down at the stable sketching horses."

Problem is, he's not actually working on Lodovico's monument at all. He's trying to come up with a proportion system for horses similar to the one he's worked out for the human body. And he's got so carried away by the bunching of muscle and the wrinkling of flesh that he's writing a treatise* for painters on the subject. I'm sure one day everyone will be very grateful to read this definitive work on

* essay.

How to Paint a Horse, but you can see my problem, can't you? He gets side-tracked so easily that NOTHING GETS FINISHED! I just hope Lodovico doesn't blame me.

Milan, December, 1493

You are not going to believe this, but the horse is ready for casting*. You won't believe the size of it either. Three-times-life-sized is a great deal bigger than it sounds. I know, because I heaved every bag of clay into the barn where it stands, and every bag of plaster that made the mould. We are just waiting for Lodovico to send over the bronze that he's had set aside for this project, and then we'll be done – a mere twelve years late.

* pouring molten metal into a mould to make a statue.

Leonardo has spent almost as much time on working out how to cast the horse as he has on sculpting the model. He's drawn details of a massive corset of iron bars and hooks to fit on the outside of the mould to stop it collapsing.

The guys from the foundry came round and scratched their heads and walked away again because, in spite of the iron corset, they can see the difficulties. The horse is supposed to be hollow, a shell four centimetres thick, but it'll still weigh sixty-five tons.

"There's another little *problema* you might like to consider, Maestro," I piped up after the foundry workers had gone home to their spaghetti. "There's the small matter of the rider."

"Who?" queried our greatest living Italian.

"The guy this monument's all about. The guy we've not done a drawing of yet or made a model of. The three-times-life-sized guy who's going to sit on this horse and crush it into the ground like tissue paper."

"Oh, him," said Leonardo, quickly picking up his sketchbook. "I knew I'd forgotten something."

Milan, November, 1494

The horse is just one big headache. I have just heard that the bronze we've been waiting for has been used to make CANNONS! So no horse. All that work for nothing. The clay model sits there like a lump, the moulds are piled up in a corner, I am distracted, Lodovico has lost all interest in art because he's too busy fighting the French, and Leonardo has gone back to drawing cathedrals. I should have got a job in a bakery.

What a waste of time all this war business is. We hear that the French have triumphantly entered Florence, but instead of fighting them, the Florentines welcomed eight hundred knights in armour, a company of archers and the French king on a black charger surrounded by a hundred bodyguards. They even took down a section of the city walls so they could march in more easily. They probably gave them all free ice-creams too.

Milan, 1495

More news from Florence – ah home, sweet home! There's been a revolution there. Some mad preacher called Savonarola has revolted on behalf of the people and publicly burnt works of art belonging to the rich, which he says are the works of the Devil. He called it the *Bonfire of the Vanities*. If he's burnt anything I've worked on, he'll know about it.

Leonardo was particularly thrilled to hear that the painting that annoyed Savonarola the most is the one in the Tornabuoni chapel that young Michelangelo had a hand in. He's a painter and sculptor who's attracting a bit too much attention for the boss's liking. Actually they're not bad frescoes, it's just that they make the Tornabuoni family look as if they're up there with God Almighty.

Here in Milan we're always at war with Venice or France, while over in Florence they are permanently at loggerheads with Pisa. Well, now apparently there's a Great Council of citizens in Florence, so the people (well, some of them) have a say in how things (mostly bonfires, I suppose) are run.

The wars are heating up a bit here, and my wife Giulia and I are trying to persuade Leonardo to consider moving.

"No horse, no point in staying," I said to him.

"Ah," he replied. "But I've just been commissioned to paint *The Last Supper* in the refectory* of the monastery of Santa Maria delle Grazie, and I'm going to start it right away."

He's working like crazy on the preliminary drawings. *The Last Supper* is to be a fresco on the end wall. It's going to be a masterpiece of perspective**, so that when the monks are eating in their refectory, they will feel like they are in the same room as Christ and his disciples.

Ambitious, but if anyone can pull it off, Leonardo da Vinci can.

* communal dining room.

** the art of painting distance and size accurately.

He is also filling notebooks with formulas for working out the way light and shade behave across the surface of an object. It all sounds too brainy for me, but Leonardo says he's trying to take the guesswork out of painting light. But that's him all over. Most artists would just get on and paint what they saw. Leonardo has to analyse and explain everything.

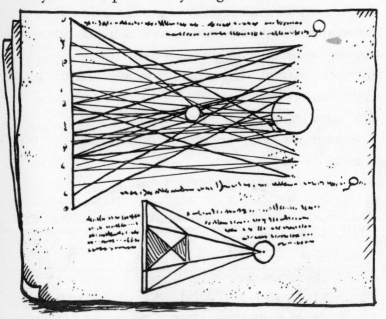

To paint a fresco you have to work fast, because you have to paint while the plaster on the wall is wet. So you get about a day to paint a section of wall, and if you make a mistake you have to put on a new layer of plaster and start again.

Working fast *and* on wet plaster, now that'll be a challenge for The Maestro!

Milan, January, 1496

Did I say working fast? Leonardo has decided to use another technique. It's called working extremely slowly on dry plaster. Leonardo's mania for invention has resulted in a new chemical mixture to stick the paint to the wall. It may work, and on the other hand it may not, but it certainly gives Leonardo plenty of time to stand around in front of his painting. He waits for inspiration and then dabs on three or four brushstrokes from time to time. I see another Sforza Horse disaster coming up.

He has been summoned to the monastery to explain the delay. You have to admire his talent for making excuses. He told them that he was waiting for inspiration from within, in order to paint the face of Jesus, which must be ideal.

What could they do but agree with him?

Milan, Spring, 1497

The Prior* of Santa Maria delle Grazie, who commissioned this work some three years ago and was hoping to have the whole thing finished in a matter of months, has started peeking through the keyhole. All he sees is Leonardo standing there, arms folded, doing nothing. He had the nerve the other day to suggest to Leonardo that he might possibly stop messing around and get a move on.

* deputy head of a monastery.

Leonardo turned slowly to look at him. "I am standing here because I am having problems imagining the face of anyone as evil as Judas." He smiled sickeningly, and continued: "If you are in a hurry, Prior, then the problem could be solved by using your face as the model."

I blended into the background and the Prior quietly left town, leaving Leonardo staring thoughtfully at his unfinished painting.

Milan, January, 1498

Well, it's finished. They look like a bunch of real people up there eating the Last Supper together, but every one of them has a distinct personality and you can tell that they've all got something different on their minds.

Leonardo is pleased with his fresco, particularly because it is so real and alive. He gave himself a pat on the back by saying to the world at large that "the most praiseworthy form of painting is the one that most resembles what it imitates." Well, it's certainly lifelike!

Milan, Winter, 1499

One of the reasons *The Last Supper* took so long was because of the book. Leonardo and Luca the mathematician have produced a book called *Divine Proportions*.

I told them straight up that the title was misleading. I mean, a man might rush out and buy a book like that, thinking it would be full of pictures of curvy girls.

How wrong they would be. It is full of geometrical shapes.

Milan, October, 1499

It's all happening here. Lodovico has been defeated. The French troops, not content with invading Milan, have broken up the clay model of the horse. I am not going to go into what I said when I heard the soldiers had used it for target practice, but it is time to go and I am packing the bags. I think we should go back to Florence. They've burnt the mad preacher Savonarola at the stake, so the city is fit for artists and their patrons once again.

Venice, December, 1499

We're on the way home to Florence, at last. Just stopped off here briefly to check out the centennial celebrations, down a skinful of Chianti and fall in a canal or two. Luca the mathematician has come with us, so there's a lot of calculating going on and not a great deal of drawing or painting.

Florence, 24th April, 1500

Well it's great to be back. I have to say that I missed the old place. I missed strolling over the Ponte Vecchio on a balmy evening, looking in all the shops built on either side. What I did not miss quite so much was being anywhere near the bridge on a hot summer's day, when all the leather workers hang out their hides and get to work soaking them in horse's urine. And the river can look pretty disgusting after the butchers, who also have shops on the bridge, have chucked their grisly offcuts into the river.

Everyone's been talking about Leonardo da Vinci, even though we've been away for seventeen years! A member of the City's art establishment has said of him, "Leonardo's mathematical experiments have so distracted him from painting that he cannot even bear to pick up a brush." He doesn't know the half of it, does he?

Florence, 1501

We have a painting! And I'm back to mixing paints! Well, at least we have the cartoon (that's the technical term for a full-size drawing) for an altarpiece of *The Virgin and Child with St Anne and a Lamb*. A bit of a clumsy title, but a wonderful composition. Leonardo paints such beautiful women, it's hard to believe he prefers scribbling in his notebooks and yattering about mathematics, but there you go. It takes all sorts.

You have to have a short memory in the art business. The painting was commissioned by Louis XII, King of France, the very man whose troops broke up our horse... GRRR... I mustn't get over-excited.

Florence, December 1501

This artist Michelangelo's making a big name for himself. Leonardo's not taking it at all well, especially as Michelangelo's done the curly-haired-young-man-with-no-clothes-on bit to perfection with his statue of *David*.

"Don't let it get to you, boss," I said. "He may be the sculpture king, but there's nobody like you on the paintbrush."

I hear from Michelangelo's chisel-sharpener that he can be as arrogant and as difficult to work for as Leonardo. He's never satisfied with anything he does either, and is another fan of the 'unfinished' look. He is known to have said, "With my mother's milk I sucked in the hammer and chisels I use for my statues." What does that make his mother? A hardware store?

Rome, 1502

The ruler in Rome is cruel and ruthless, and he's called Cesare Borgia. He makes the Devil himself seem like a pussycat. Borgia, who thinks Leonardo is the world's greatest military engineer, has invited The Maestro to Rome to help build defences in the province of Romagna*. It is the kind of invitation one does not turn down.

Needless to say, Leonardo is thrilled. That's because he'd rather be sketching machinery than painting beautiful women. I do not think Signore Borgia can have heard about Leonardo's design for the armoured car, and I'm certainly not going to mention it. The truth about The Maestro's works of engineering is that they look great in theory, but no one knows how to build them!

* principal city Bologna, the home of Spaghetti Bolognese.

Leonardo gets quite worked up about death and destruction, and loves conjuring up battle scenes for the entertainment of his patrons. They love it too, of course. When he's flipping through his sketchbooks and showing off his murderous inventions, he makes quite a performance of it.

Naturally, I have to go along and help. His instructions to me are to read, and I quote here: "in a frenzied or berserk manner as in mental lunacy."

"My job is to mix paints," I protest feebly.

Imola (near Bologna), 1503

We have made Signore Borgia a map. A wonderful map of Imola, which is apparently a very important town in his battle plans. I can't tell you the amount of work involved. We had a surveying disc covered in lines and numbers to measure the height of all the buildings. And guess who had to pace out the distances between every house on every street? Then Leonardo put all the information together and coloured it all in. Imola now has the best map of any town in the world, and I have blisters on my feet.

My job is to mix paints.

Pisa, March 1503

Florence is at war with Pisa, and here we are building canals in the thick of battle. The drawings have been done of course, and on paper it looks dead simple: just change the course of the River Arno so that Pisa no longer has access to the sea. Digging has started, but neither the sea nor the river are being very co-operative. I have blisters on my hands now.

My job is to mix paints.

Florence, October 1503

A commission for a mural in the Palazzo Vecchio! This is more like it: this is art. They want a painting of the *Battle of Anghiari* for the Council Chamber. This is to celebrate the victorious Florentine Republic, and this is just the kind of painting that makes reputations.

More sketches. This time it is trees. But it's never enough for him just to draw a tree. He's now working on the ultimate theory of the proportion of branches to trunks, and writing pages and pages on *How to Paint Trees.* Guess who gets to climb up the tree with the tape measure?

Florence, November 1503

Before making a start on the mural, Leonardo has got involved in another canal scheme. This one is on behalf of the Wool Weavers' Guild. Let me just explain how important they are, dear Diary, before you start thinking "Huh! What does a bunch of woolly-headed weavers want with a canal?"

All of Florence's flourishing wealth is based on the Guild system. Guilds are rich and powerful groups set up to control trade and politics. The seven major Guilds that run the city of Florence are:

1. Cloth merchants
2. Wool weavers
3. Silk weavers and goldsmiths
4. Furriers
5. Lawyers
6. Bankers
7. Doctors, sellers of pigments and artists.

There are fourteen minor Guilds representing tradesmen, but poor old fishmongers and farm labourers have to struggle along without Guild backing.

The plan is to join Florence to the sea by a canal rather than the twisting, turning River Arno. The Wool Weavers' Guild would then get even richer and more powerful by charging everyone to use their canal.

The only *problema* is that it won't work. Leonardo knew it all along, so he handed over the drawings with a little warning to the engineers that "the river must be tempted from its course, and not treated harshly with violence." The Wool Weavers' Guild obviously thought better of this scheme and filed it away under 'I' for Impossible.

Florence, 1504

I don't know which one of them is worse, I honestly don't. I was having a tankard or two of Chianti with Michelangelo's chisel-sharpener the other day, and he showed me some Madonnas they'd been working on. Dead spitting images of Leonardo's lovely ladies, only in marble.

Typical.

Florence, June 1505

You may be wondering how the battle mural painting went. Don't ask. He did all the roughs, all the sketches, and he was just starting work on the wall when... they announced that Michelangelo had been commissioned to paint another battle scene in the same room!

It was like putting two fighting cats in a basket. In one corner is Leonardo, refusing to be hurried and trying to find yet another way to stick paint to dry plaster (I have to report that *The Last Supper* is already looking a little flaky). And in the opposing corner is Michelangelo, painting efficiently and quickly on his section of wet plaster and showing off like mad. This project is doomed.

Leonardo's battle scene is looking good. There are trampling horses and grimacing warriors and it's hard to tell whose legs and arms and hooves are whose. I think the warriors are actually making faces at Michelangelo. It doesn't help that Michelangelo is younger than Leonardo and has more of his career ahead of him.

florence, August 1505

Leonardo thinks men can fly!! He calls it the Second World of Nature. I call it total madness.

He says that if we understand how insects and birds fly and apply the same principles to a human being, then men can fly.

"But birds are built in a different way to humans," I pointed out. (Sometimes even geniuses need to be told the obvious.)

"Aha! But I can do something about that," he replied, digging out his notebooks again.

He rides up into the hills on his horse, saddlebags bulging with notebooks, pens and inks, and he's up there for hours – right through the heat of the day, when most sensible Florentine gentlemen are having a quiet snooze in the shade. That man can draw, draw, draw all day.

He first found inspiration for his flying machines in watching dragonflies. He drew a spiral air-screw with four giant wings, but that didn't look right.

Now he's working on birds. I can't tell you how many dead birds we have lying around the studio. He spends his days out in the hills watching the birds soaring about in the heavens, and his nights in the studio cutting them up to find out how they work.

Now he's drawing a pair of massive wings that are supposed to glide on air currents, and the poor guy strapped underneath this contraption is supposed to flap the wings by pushing rods with his arms and pedals with his feet.

"It's going to weigh tons," I said.

"You wouldn't complain about the weight of your wings if you were an eagle," replied my esteemed boss.

"But eagles' wings aren't made of thick wooden struts and pulleys, creaking leather joints and hefty metal springs," I replied.

Leonardo huffed and puffed and went back to the drawing board. I think there's some way to go, but it's a great idea. I'd love to fly.

Florence, December 1505

I've cleared away all the feathers and bits of dead
bird, and the studio looks almost like a painter's
studio again. Which is just as well, as we have a
lady coming round to sit for a portrait. Her
name is Signora Giacondo.

Signora
GIACONDO

She has quite a twinkle in her eye. "Just call me
Mona Lisa, dearie," she smiled when I took her
a glass of wine. She and Leonardo seem to get
on quite well. This is a good thing, as I think we
all know how long this portrait may take. I did
have a quiet word in his ear, as I know a bit
more about women than he does and I was quite
sure she would want to be painted now, in the
bloom of her youth, rather than in the blurring
of her middle age.

Leonardo gave me one of his most withering looks and replied: "Painters do not paint as a gardener digs a garden, Luigi. Men of genius are doing most when they seem to be doing least." And so saying he gazed out of the window for the rest of the afternoon and then went home.

Milan, May 1506

Leonardo has been invited back to Milan by the French governor, Charles d'Amboise. The French seem to be in a bit of a stew about an altarpiece commissioned about fourteen years ago by the Church of Santo Francesco Grande called *The Virgin of the Rocks*. It will, like all Leonardo's works, be wonderful when it is finished.

Milan, June 1506

Drawings, drawings, drawings! He draws all day long. Then I've got to find some place to store all this stuff. Moan, moan. I'll tell you why his paintings never get finished. He won't make a start until he's drawn everything from every possible angle.

Take *Leda and the Swan* for instance. This is a painting that the French King fancies hanging on the wall of his bathroom. Now Leonardo has drawn Leda's head I don't know how many times. You would expect that. What you might not expect is that he's also drawn her head from the back.

This is typical Leonardo, so you see what I'm up against.

"Maybe the French King would rather have the painting this year," I suggested feebly, "instead of waiting until he's died of old age while you work out what the back of her head looks like, especially when it doesn't even appear in the picture!"

Leonardo sighed patiently and proceeded to lecture me on the fact that as he'd given Leda a wig of coiled and plaited hair, it was obviously very important to know how the wig fitted at the back.

"Okay, okay," I said as I re-filled his inkwell, "keep your hair on!"

florence, 1508

Leonardo is trying to figure out how eyes work. He's fiddling about with a black box with a little hole in it called a camera obscura, and is obsessed with a) the idea of images passing through darkness and b) capturing still frames of motion. He'll be making moving pictures next.

Meanwhile, the portrait of Mona Lisa smiles at us in all its unfinished glory from the corner of the studio. That smile certainly gets you. While she was sitting for it, Leonardo told Signora Giaconda jokes and recited verses, and he would bring her bunches of flowers and other little surprises to keep her face lively and animated.

And there's something else about that picture too. It's that coming-at-you-out-of-the-shadows thing. It's as if he's painted with light and shade instead of a paintbrush. Everyone who sees it is gobsmacked.

Milan, 1508

We have to keep travelling back and forth from Florence to Milan in order to finish various paintings. Leonardo has been talent-spotted by that horse vandal, the French King Louis XII.

He wants lots of Leonardo's paintings, but seems just as interested in his other activities in the fields of mechanical engineering. The king called him "our dear and beloved Leonardo, our painter and engineer," and Leonardo couldn't have been more pleased. Especially as he hasn't been asked to go to Rome and paint the ceiling of the Sistine Chapel – that job has gone to young Michelangelo, about whom the least said in front of Leonardo the better.

Florence, September 1508

All this praise from the French Court has gone to Leonardo's head. He is now determined to become the world's greatest anatomist, or cutter-up and recorder of dead bodies.

He was hanging around the Santa Maria Nova hospital when an old man of 100 breathed his last the other day. Leonardo decided it would be a good idea to cut up the old man's body to find out what happens as the human body ages.

Dead bodies smell terrible. Why can't he draw flowers and fruit like everybody else?

Old men, young men, pregnant women, babies. Show Leonardo a dead body and he's in there with his pen and ink faster than you can say *yeeeucchhh!* He's worked out the way muscles attach to bone and the way blood whooshes round in our veins.

"Sight and insight, that's what you need, Luigi," he said to me on the way to the mortuary.

"I'll settle for a clothes peg," said I.

He knows so much about the way the human body works that he'd make a great doctor. In fact, I'd rather have him tend to me if I got sick than some of the so-called doctors you see practising on patients in the marketplace. You see them doing unmentionable things with red-hot pokers, rubbing their patients with crushed chickpeas and prescribing liberal applications of pigeon dung for bad cases of dandruff.

Florence, 1509

Drapes, drapes, drapes! He's obsessed with
drapery now. I sat there all day Monday
swathed in silk while he drew the layers and
folds. Tuesday I thought I might nip up into the
hills and snare a few rabbits for tea, but oh no!
Forget Luigi's day off. It was velvet on Tuesday,
fine linen on Wednesday, coarse linen on
Thursday and he's got a full week planned for
cottons.

And why? I'll tell you why in his own words: "By nature everything has a desire to remain as it is. Drapery strives to lie flat. When it is forced into pleats or folds, observe the effect of the strain on that part which is most bunched up."

"You could drape a bit of sacking over a chair and observe it straining away all day long," I grumbled.

"Ah Luigi!" replied The Maestro. "Cloths of different kinds display different fold patterns, and the folds respond to the motion of the figures."

I am only writing this down so that if anyone is peeking through the window of our studio and sees me flitting from side to side wearing nothing but a wisp of muslin, they will know that a) it wasn't my idea and b) it is all in the cause of art.

Milan, 1510

Back in Milan now. I get the odd letter from Mona Lisa wondering what's happened to her portrait. I sent her back a note saying not to fret, one day it would be completed and hers would be the most famous face in the history of painting. That might keep her quiet for another couple of years. Meanwhile he's knocked up a *fabuloso* picture of *St John the Baptist* for the French King.

Milan, 1511

Rocks, rocks, rocks! It's out with the red chalk and he's drawing rock formations all day.

When I suggested it might be an idea to finish off *Mona Lisa*, he said he was working on it the way all geniuses do. "I think I might put some rocks in the background of her portrait," he said. "On the other hand, I might not."

Milan, June 1512

Little bit of a change of plan in Milan. It no longer belongs to the French, but to the combined forces of Spain, the Pope and Venice. Time to pack the bags again – we've been invited to go to Rome and meet Pope Leo X, who turns out to be Giovanni de Medici, so we know the family well.

Have I mentioned Francesco Melzi? He's a very nice boy. Lives just outside Milan in the Villa Melzi, and he's been studying with Leonardo for a while as his pupil. Francesco has invited Leonardo to stay for a bit. Apparently there are a lot of rocks around the Villa Melzi so Leonardo didn't wait to be asked twice.

Rome, December 1513

Well here we are in Rome (Melzi has come too), installed in a very nice apartment in the Vatican Palace courtesy of the Pope's brother Giuliano, who is conveniently also the head of the Florentine State.

Leonardo was summoned to see the Pope the other day. I think he was expecting at the very least a commission for an altarpiece, and at the most, a brief to design a revolutionary new cathedral, but all he got was a lecture on using corpses for his anatomical studies.

I think even Leonardo knows better than to argue with the Pope.

Rome, 1513

I have to say that Leonardo does look older than he is. I mean, he's in his sixties, but some unkind soul remarked that he looks well over seventy. This is something that Leonardo encourages, I think. Now that his vigorous youth and his productive middle years are past, he likes to think of himself as a venerable old man who could perhaps be compared in wisdom and creativity to God the Father. This is certainly the way he draws himself.

LEONARDO
VINCI

He's drawing all kinds of swirling lines that look like a great flood swamping the earth at the moment. Has he been having visions of the end of the world? Is it a reaction to the violent storms in the Alps that everyone's talking about? Has he been eating too much cheese before bedtime?

I'm calling them the Deluge Drawings. And I think I've worked out what they're all about. He's trying to make the forces of Nature into patterns he can understand. That and the fact that he's been studying the movement of water for so long (don't mention the canals) means he wants to show off what's he learned.

Rome, 1514

There's not much for Leonardo to do here. His notebooks are full of mirrors, mechanics, geometry puzzles and a few drawings of cathedrals (just in case anyone should call round wanting one). He's got the architecture bug quite seriously now that architecture has become an art in its own right with rules and geometry and mathematics. (There was a time when all you had to do to be an architect was draw a pretty picture and hope some builder would come up with a clever way of making it stand up.)

But no one is going to pull down the Vatican and start again, and the result is that *Mona Lisa* is finally finished. And yes, there are some rocks in the background.

Rome, 1515

Now there's something to do. The Medici Pope is visiting his home town of Florence as the most powerful ruler of all Italy, and every Florentine artist imaginable is involved in the festivities.

Leonardo has done some costume designs for the pageant, so the studio is once again full of curly-haired young men in feathered caps and fetching tights.

Rome, March 1516

Our host, the Pope's brother, is dead, so we're moving again. Leonardo is quite pleased about this, because there's nothing he'd like better than to get back under the patronage of the French King François I.

François came to the throne last year and, like his predecessor Louis XII, thinks Leonardo is just *magnifique*. Apparently François told another member of the Colourful Set that he (and I quote, so don't blame me for his sentence construction): "did not believe that a man had been born who knew as much as Leonardo, not only in the spheres of painting, sculpture and architecture, but also that he was a very great philosopher."

Everyone worships Leonardo now. All the other painters like Titian and Raphael agree that he changed things. He was the first (and the best) at painting people with subtle expressions on their faces so you could almost tell what they were thinking.

Château de Cloux, Amboise, Northern France, April 1516

François I, the King of France, knows how to treat a court painter. And what's more, he knows how to treat Leonardo. He's not asking for altarpieces or frescoes. He just wants old Leonardo to work away at his geometry, live in this very pretty Château in the Loire valley with his friend Francesco Melzi, design the odd theatrical costume and work out ways to force the River Loire into canals. Leonardo has a smile from ear to ear. It is a great way to end his career.

Amboise, October 1517

We've just had a visit from the Cardinal of Aragon. He's a bit of an unobservant old prune. He told his secretary that, impressed as he was by Leonardo's magnificent paintings: "Nothing more that is fine can be expected of him, owing to the paralysis which has attacked his right hand."

What he doesn't know is that *numero uno*, Leonardo is left-handed, and *numero due*, Leonardo would much rather draw and write and design drainage systems than paint an altarpiece.

Amboise, May 2, 1519

Leonardo died today, at the age of sixty-seven.
He died in the arms of the French King,
François I. That's pretty good for the illegitimate
son of a peasant girl from Vinci.

Before everyone else gets their tributes in, I want to put in mine. The man was a genius who always wanted to find out more. He wanted to know how the world worked, and that is what kept him going. He was not a man to mess with, he was always the boss, he always knew better than anyone else, and I think he would rather be remembered as a philosopher of great intellect than a painter of beautiful pictures. And yet, I bet you anything you like that Mona Lisa's little smile will be the thing that people will remember him by, hundreds of years from now.

Leonardo has left everything to Francesco Melzi. Melzi is going to have an enormous job on his hands, cataloguing and sorting through all those drawings and sketchbooks, the writings and the zillion and one half-finished projects.

As it is, we are left with thirteen finished paintings, a flaking mural in the monastery at Santa Maria delle Grazie, and the drawings and manuscripts of a man who had so many ideas that it would take twenty lifetimes to complete them all.

PUBLISHER'S ADDENDUM

Alex Parsons' story about finding this diary in an Italian restaurant is a little hard to believe. Lengthy researches have failed to track down evidence for the existence of Leonardo's paint mixer, and forensic analysis of the 'age spots' on the pages of the diary have been found to contain traces of tomato purée.

However, there are some things we can be sure of. Leonardo's character and the details of his life and works do actually check out. In fact, they were checked out by Casey Parsons (thank you Casey), who is no slouch himself when it comes to making a good spaghetti sauce.

P.S.

In 1990, one hundred and fifty art historians and engineers got together to see if it might be possible to build the Sforza horse after all, following Leonardo's very detailed drawings and instructions. What they found was not encouraging. Even if all four legs were on the ground, they couldn't possibly hold the weight, and a casting that large would never cool evenly so the metal would crack. It is impossible to know how Leonardo planned to overcome these problems, given the technology available to him at the time.

Japanese engineers have built a full-scale Sforza horse, but out of fibreglass, which is cheating really. American engineers are now creating an authentic Sforza horse by casting a thin bronze skin in ten pieces and assembling it over a stainless steel skeleton. America will then give the completed Horse to Italy in recognition of all that Italian culture has given to America. It will be unveiled in Milan on September 10, 1999, exactly 500 years after Milan was invaded and Leonardo's clay model of the horse was destroyed.

Order Form

To order direct from the publishers, just make a list of the titles you want and fill in the form below:

Name ....

Address ....

....

....

Send to: Dept 6, HarperCollins Publishers Ltd, Westerhill Road, Bishopbriggs, Glasgow G64 2QT.

Please enclose a cheque or postal order to the value of the cover price, plus:

UK & BFPO: Add £1.00 for the first book, and 25p per copy for each additional book ordered.

Overseas and Eire: Add £2.95 service charge. Books will be sent by surface mail but quotes for airmail despatch will be given on request.

A 24-hour telephone ordering service is available to holders of Visa, MasterCard, Amex or Switch cards on 0141- 772 2281.

Collins
An *Imprint of* HarperCollins*Publishers*